the SHORT of it...

H. William Ruback

Copyright

the SHORT of it…: is an anthology of fiction. Names, characters, places, and incidents either are products of the author's imagination or are used fictitiously. Any resemblance to actual events or locales or persons, living or dead, is entirely coincidental.

Cover design by © 2014 H. William Ruback
Front Cover Photo : © Valeriy Gayevyy @123rf.com
Back Cover Photo :
© Aleksandr Steblovskiy @123rf.com

Published in the United States 2014
by

ARGON PRESS

www.ArgonPress.com

the SHORT of it…

“an accessible sophistication that you cannot find in fiction today.”

“a delightful and diverse potpourri...”

“Every soul who looks upon Ruback’s words will no doubt find a mirror on the page reflecting their own emotions back at them.”

“At times it brings to mind what Lovecraft would sound like if he was writing from a post-modern perspective and had a sense of humour.”

“I read and re-read his words many times, each time seeing different things and taking away different moanings.”

“There is something for everyone within!”

Dedication

Always for:
D.C.R. and B.A.R.
And Forever
E.A.R. and R.K.R.

And for my Little Darling

Special consideration for all of the amazing folks at ArgonPress whose hard work has truly given new life to my writing ambitions.

Thank You!

also to new discoveries, those brought with them, and the inspirations and corrections that have made the stories inside, that much better: Thank You Helle and Jen

Introduction

... a dim desk lamp glared heavily on the eyes of a weary young man. The countless hours, days, behind the desk seemed to have taken its toll... but there was still life left in the hand that held the pen. A glimmer of adventure and a spark of determination left in the tired mind.

The sun was creeping over the horizon adding a poetic backdrop to the chirping of the birds. Their morning cry had begun nearly two hours earlier.

"No perception of time, it was only five a.m. now."

A glimpse over the shoulder, to the window, then across the room, his view was drawn to the not so silent figure of his sleeping companion. Big and furry, his body often lent warmth to his master's cold feet.

"You should feel how soft he is."

The pen was set down, as a smile beamed across his face. The young writer finished his first story.

The adrenalin surge was enormous. He felt like screaming, shouting, he wanted his pleasure known to everyone around him.

Silence.

Didn't matter though, the self gratification would last for a long time to come...

#

... there is no one direction that my writing has focused upon. An idea can be born from a single thought, word or image. Often times the end result no longer resembles the original concept. I would hope that the final product would need no explanation, but just in case, on occasion, it couldn't hurt.

en'koun(t)ər

This story is a twist on an old account of my family history, but it was born from a writing exercise. Given a photo from a magazine, I was tasked to write a fictional tale based on the inspiration of that image. Its location, Denmark, made the rest a fore-gone conclusion. The only thing I wasn't sure of, was what to call it…

In My Blood
or
History Repeats
or
Following in the Footsteps of My Forefathers

What the hell am I doing in Denmark?

I have to keep asking myself this same question over and over again. Then maybe I'll figure out the answer.

Here I sit in some little, insignificant restaurant, in an even smaller town. I think it's called the Odense, Altes Gasthaus. Whether that's the restaurant's name or the town's, I just don't know anymore. They tell me that it's the third largest city in

Denmark, but I'd swear there are more people in my apartment building back home.

It has been quite some time since I last gave in to one of my flights of fancy. The last was a three-week trek through the Amazon, just to research a short story. After my head cleared from the fever and bout of malaria, I couldn't even remember what I wanted to write about.

But that was yesterday and this is today.

No! This is crazy!

Several years ago when I began my illustrious career as a writer, I decided to use my resources to research my family tree. Hoping to find that one link that connected myself to a great past or person. A similar wish that many had had before, no doubt.

A family tree is a little harder to grow than a two hundred foot redwood, and it takes just about as long. So it isn't hard to imagine that I did not progress, or should that be regress, that far.

Of course my immediate relatives were easy to track down. All it took was a phone and about ten minutes. It's when I started progressing, or is that digressing, that I began to have a little difficulty. It turned out that my great, great, great someone or other sold them-selves into slavery in order to get passage across from Europe. When they reached the promised land of America, they booked and took up refuge in the northern Midwest. So! There really weren't a whole hell of a lot of documents to document the lineage.

Anyway, I digress… I think I got that one right.

After some time I did manage though, to track down yet another grandfather of the past. (I hate using all of those greats. My editor would think that I put them in just to pad my word count.) It was said, that he happened to be a member of the Danish Aristocracy.

Which is, I guess, why I am now sitting in this insignificant restaurant in this tiny city somewhere just east of Copenhagen and west of no-where.

I was intrigued by my apparent noble bloodline and was ready to return to claim some lost inheritance of power, when the story took a sharp turn right off the edge of a cliff. It seems that my relative was disowned by his noble family for some minor indiscretion…

Okay. He married the maid.

End of inheritance. End of story.

Except here I sit in the Odense, Altes Gasthaus, sipping on some disgustingly warm ale that they try to pass off as beer. (Man could I go for a Miller Genuine Draft right about now.) I guess I really can't complain though, the town and its people are as warm as their ale and not quite so disgusting.

The scenery, now that I take time to notice, is quite charming. The mosaic pattern of the cobblestone catches every facet of the sunlight. And I must confess the architecture is beautiful. Across the road are several houses all built in a similar style. Their facings, whether it be brick or cement, were all tapered floor by floor, giving each the appearance of looking like a pyramid. The angled steps leading up to their round archways lent a sharp contrast to the multitude of windows that covered the entire front of each building.

As the sun slowly passed across a particular building I caught the movement of a figure in one of the windows. Now mind you, I don't prescribe to be a peeping tom by nature, but there was something in the way she looked. Something in the way she moved that, that… I just can't describe it.

A writer at a loss for words isn't a pretty sight to behold.

She was though. Even through the window her features radiated. The sun sparkled in her eyes and set that long blond hair aflame. There seemed to be a melody in her movement as she glided from one window to the other. By the tilt of her head and the silent movement of her mouth, I could tell that she was, indeed, singing. Though I couldn't hear one note, I could feel the tune.

I got lost in that song and before I knew it, my overactive imagination had me engaged in the most glorious of fantasies.

The waitress' inquiring as to my well-being, in her labored English brought me back to reality. I smiled and made some gesture and comment about the local ale, which seemed to satisfy her. She walked away with that smile that said, "What the hell did you just say, you stupid foreigner?"

Once my anger at her interruption had subsided, I again turned my gaze to the vision across the street, only to see every window vacant.

Damn!

I threw more obscenities in the direction of the waitress just to alleviate my anger at having lost sight of that gorgeous creature.

Turning again to look out the window, my heart skipped a beat at the sight of the door opening.

Could my luck actually be this good?

Yes and no.

It was her alright, in all of her splendor, but…

I seemed to have failed to notice her mode of dress and the apparent reason for her movement throughout the building. As she stood there in her black skirt and white blouse, waving the broom back and forth across the stairs. I felt one hundred years of history flash through my head. I couldn't believe it.

A maid.

Now I realize that that shouldn't have held any bearing on the fact that I found her to be one of the loveliest creatures ever to grace this planet, but it did.

I stared at her. Not because of her charm, because of my disbelief. I quickly realized my ignorant behavior and turned my head. Not quickly enough though, I couldn't avoid her glance and beaming smile.

As I sat there staring at my now hot ale, yuk, my heart started a wild roller-coaster ride inside my chest.

Up! She smiled at me. She loves me.

Down. She's a maid. No way in hell am I going to fall into that ancestral trap.

And while my heart and mind went for a ride through an emotional Disneyland, I failed to notice her departure. When I finally came to grips with the situation, I looked again… She was gone.

Again. *Damn!*

Wait, she's not gone, I can still see the image of her face, like a reflection in the glass.

Her voice was like music. It actually took my haggard mind a quick moment to figure out that it was not her reflection, but actually that she was standing beside me. Again she greeted me with her soft accented English and asked if it would be all right to share the view. Only the only vision was the one in front of me. Her.

I said of course, of course and she sat. And we talked and talked. I even began to enjoy the taste of that fine warm ale.

To this day, we sit at that same table every time we return to Denmark. And each time, I raise a glass of ale and toast my great, great, grandfather.

Desire

desires of the Mind, pleasures of the Flesh
when do they Divide, when they Meet
know what you Want, receive what you Deserve
Call upon others, but know when to Serve
seek out their Weakness, but conquer through their Strength
always think of Distance, but never go the Length
love until Broken, Mend what you find
open to Receive, let bodies Entwine

There I Go Again

I thought that I should tell you,
all the things you wanted to hear.
I thought that there would be laughter
and joy to cover the tears.
I thought the truth would somehow
hurt,
even more than all the lies.
I thought and then thought better,
for the answer was in your eyes.
Of honesty and reality, though they
pain,
I think them best.
To achieve trust and reach sensitivity,
only then does love past the test.

Immaterial Disguise

I couldn't help but feel as if I knew this woman from someplace else, from another time in both of our lives. And yet, there was really nothing familiar about her at all. The smile that arced across her lips seemed wicked in a way that I couldn't describe. Her eyes were deep and haunting, yet I found myself entranced by the pale glow of their color.

I tried not to look in her direction. Tried not to be overtly obvious with my leering glances. But she knew the affect she was having on my libido, and she reveled in the moment. Taunting me, setting me up for that one instance when I would let my overconfidence get the better of me. For that moment that I would summon up enough courage to walk up to her and stare into those intense, blue eyes and say… something completely asinine.

Her response would be short, totally polite, and yet it would hold all of the venomous thunder that one human being could possibly direct at another. And as I would dejectedly turn and walk back to my seat, she would turn to her friends and laugh aloud at the demoralizing blow that she had struck me with.

And that was exactly the way it happened.

"Ah! What a lovely day for romance!"

~#~

It wasn't until many hours and several pints of alcohol later, that her cruel joke would take total effect, though. As the bar stood quiet, except for the last scurrying dialog of its final patrons as they exited the establishment, a soft and lilting voice sang to me.

Her bold bravado, now gone, lost with the departure of her pristine, celluloid comrades, now became the sound of a compassionate human being. One who was just as afraid as I to spend yet another night alone and cold.

The owner's beckoning to exit his establishment repeatedly interrupted our conversation and we found ourselves cringing from the harshness of the winter air, outside. Our breath spat columns of mist as we spoke the foolish ritual of first encounters. All of this, leading up to the final question: would we be alone tonight, or would we entangle ourselves into each other's lives?

~#~

Hours later, with the heat of passion subsiding, we lay in each other's arms oblivious to the other's thoughts and concerns. Caring not for the other's mutual fulfillment or emotional well-being. Just reflecting upon and dissecting the moments passed. Searching for our own gratification, and wondering if a continuation of this relationship would be beneficial to our-selves.

Sleep, having overcome us hours ago, now passes into the waking of another day. The waking of new complications. Of answering questions we're not prepared to answer. Even though we spent half of the night pondering on them.

We play the lover's dance and exchange pleasantries and playful volleys of conversation. The future nothing more than the clouded vision of yet another smoke filled room.

Will we say our good-byes, for now, not knowing of the direction we are headed in, if at all? Not knowing if either will be willing to make the first concession and bring truth into view.

Or will we part company still wearing the same immaterial disguises we wore the night before?

'lejən,derē

Mandrake; Me

"...there was a time you know... yes, there was a time," he paused as a worried expression came over his weathered face. "A time when memory and imagination would combine to construct reality. Hmmm... a time, yes a time."

I had to look away, for I caught myself getting lost in those words, lost in the lines of that aged face. It was haunting not realizing, no, not understanding what pain and agony this man had gone through.

Oh, I realized certain stories of his past were true, and you could almost pick out the ones that crept out of that beaten imagination. But when he spoke, as he was now, you stopped trying to decipher reality from fantasy. God! You almost stopped breathing altogether.

Those words filtered through your very being... and then you came down again.

I wiped my head and there was an enormous amount of perspiration, as there always was after one of our sessions. I felt totally drained and by the looks of the slumped over figure, he was too.

It was almost as if he were dead, that for a brief moment the corpse had awakened just to give one last soliloquy of a dying entity.

Expressions faded. The lines seemed to ease their pull on the dried out skin… a passive deluge.

I walked the streets, deserted by nightfall. Wandering aimlessly, my destination and the direction of home clouded by my thoughts.

As much as I tried, I couldn't for the life of me remember what day it was. I seemed to remember daylight, then passing, then daylight and passing again, but how long had it really been since last I was away from this Mandrake? And furthermore, when had I first arrived?

Time slipping by so quickly…

I can't even remember how I had met this old soul, but, now that the introduction was made, I found it increasingly difficult to spend any time away from him.

I fumbled for the keys to my apartment. Switching on the light, I stumbled over an immense pile of mail that had collected at the base of the door. The air was heavy and dust covered everything.

Time slipping…

My head swam with dizziness as I sank into the couch, losing all sense of consciousness.

"Only by revealing oneself to others can we begin to understand and learn about one's self."

I watched as his animated expressions and gestures ripped the very heart out of his chest.

"We must show true expression, no more should we conceal. In deceit there is only pain and torment. In truth we find serenity and understanding. We can not learn through lies, they only cloud the visions."

Always I found myself in the position to push further, to question him more, to sink deeper and of this he was waiting. Expecting my questions. Elated when finally I did… and dejected when I was satisfied and left it as is.

"What visions?"

"The visions of the Mages, held together by a single thread… Truth…Through truth a mage can see past and present, reality and beyond, for his eyes and through the eyes of others."

"But what of the future?"

"Ahh! The future is predicted, but, uncertain. One cannot see along a thread that does not exist.

Too many doubts lay in wait… And vision is only through certainty."

He paused…

... and then, that dejected expression overcame him and I knew that "we" had made an error. An error in judgment. Not in practice. But I knew not what else to ask except why was it always "We"? We this. We that. But always no answer, just that look.

The more I sat enveloped in his life. Mine seemed to disappear. All past started fading, the blur to be replaced by his visions of centuries past.

Conceived of the earth at the beginning, existing always and yet from time to time, not at all. Held in check by the elements of the earth. Allowed to act only when the whimsical world demanded. Always present in the eye of the storm, and symmetrical with the peace and calm of the summer solstice.

I sat once again, staring at the form. Each line, crease and wrinkle tracing the roads through history. Each one becoming increasingly familiar.

A furrowed brow, leading to those eyes…

The gleam in those eyes telling a story…

Each story becoming the reality it once was…

Night fell again.

His head lifted and those eyes sparked a flame

into the dark.

A single candle was lit. The small wavering flame cast a warm glow to his genteel grey eyes.

A sort of beckoning to mind and body.

I felt the constant pull of mind leaving body. I was suddenly aware of all that surrounded me. It wasn't the same room that I had spent countless hours in. Now it was clear, very clear!

Hand carved tables and chairs covered in faded velvet, piled with leather bound books, each with pages yellowed and brittle…

A hall of scrolls and tablets, old, weathered, their satin bindings almost crumbling to dust…

Crystal balls with their prisms of light, glimmering on their stands of deformed branches, twisted, with bark split and peeling…

The gloom of the dark, cold and crumbling stone walls, made my head swim. Their dullness pounding somber fate at my temples.

The acrid scent of the air, stale from decay, with an overpowering stench, seemingly, coming from… yes, a stable.

I walked further down the hall. A window niche was ornamented by metal spears with points so sharp…

But wait!

Not a spear! A tail! The end of a dragon's tail, smoked black and charred, forged almost as a sword would have been. Above the center window hung a claw, protruding its razor sharp talon toward any onlooker.

I felt increasingly faint. My head screamed. I lunged at the nearest wall for support, only to find the hollow spiraling of a staircase. Darkness engulfed my body as I fell into oblivion…

His voice broke the void.

My eyes snapped painfully open.

I was back!

Back, seated across from him once more. My body ached, pain shot through my back. Scratches and bruises covered my once flaying limbs. The staircase was a dream, but the aftermath of my fall was an all too painful reality.

"Wounds heal with time, hearts with love and caring. Oh! But a mind, a mind with only more knowledge and sensibility. A displacement of love and time."

Then, that look.

But for me… No understanding. No love. No time to heal the wounds.

Slowly they came, over and over. The words flowed past dried, hardened and cracked lips. As I sat there, hour after hour, day after day, listening, wondering, learning mage art, I realized that in this tattered room sat face-to-face teacher and student. Wizard and apprentice. I didn't ask for it, and yet, here I was, hypnotized by those grey eyes, sinking deeper and deeper into his spell.

"There will come a time…again…when man cares not of the past. When he does not understand the present and all of his fears will lie in wait of the future. When through foolishness he fears the night and the abominations the sunset will bring. The Mage Art shall return to pacify the laboured breath of the common man. To subdue the fear of the dragon, to replace tranquility in the heart, so that a few shall rise above the turmoil, and progress, and future shall bring about the Dragon's Song for Mages."

His head dropped again. Several strands of his long white hair slowly fell to cover his eyes. I knew that he was tired, but with all that I had seen and all that I had heard of his fabled future and past… it caused me to question him further. And with that question his eyes sparked new flame, the fire of exhilaration and of horrific remembrance.

"The Dragon's Song for Mages?... A cry!" he shouted. The explosion of his voice and the shrilling of the air screamed into my brain.

I felt the pain and the suffering of the dying. The lost hope of knowing the end had arrived. I saw the torment of failure, in the eyes of the creature that devoured those feelings and used them against those souls, only to add more anguish.

I saw those eyes,

fire,

black fire,

staring into my very being. Eyes that hungered for my heart. The heart that pumped the pounding blood…pounding, twisting, pulsing through my veins only causing more pain…

Unbearable pain.

I clutched my skull, ripping at my temples.

The pain!

The unbearable pain…

"A whisper."

His voice and the air calmed. The stillness and softness of my surroundings eased my tired body. Tears of pain streaked down my face.

Then the notes… Oh, those sweet notes! Touching mind and body, releasing all of the pain and suffering. Easing all tension. Replacing it with total serenity.

The Dragon's song floated through the air and yet didn't pierce the silence. The humming of their gold, singing, singing…

His voice replaced the song.

"Dragons and mages are one in the same, be it in their nature and existence. Created of the age by the fires of the earth. To restore and balance all things."

A laugh, a cynical laugh.

"No love was ever lost by a dragon for the sake of a mage. Oh no!"

And yet another laugh.

"And yet, even when the dragon swallows the heart of a mage, or one of its own for that matter… the song is heard. Mother Earth crying for one of her own."

The time to be taught had passed several weeks ago. Now it seemed that all we did these days was to stare at each other, through each other, within each other. Very seldom was a word spoken.

A short question.

A quick response. Simple, direct, but holding the deepest and truest of meanings.

And as it was in past, it was to be now, the test of all lessons. Time to show if anything had been learned.

"What has been shown?" His lips moved almost in slow motion, forcefully forming those words.

I answered, "experience through the ages."

An eruption.

"Must you be so subtle as to try and hide your ignorance and inability to comprehend these teachings? There is no shield against idiocy. Illuminate your thoughts! Bring about that change! Bring the sensibility, the truth, and the insight, that which is your being. Again I ask. What has been shown!"

The sharpness of his attack cut through my hesitancies. I had to answer. I had no choice, no will of my own. I spoke, spoke words alien to me and yet, no others would be true.

"A reverence to Time and Space. The acts of intention; to hold Mother Earth at all cost. Life and limb expendable. To relinquish evil at lengths from the Dragon's soul. To extend thine own soul as an umbrella for the protection of the misguided children, Mother Earth protecting her own."

There was an eerie pause as he tapped at his upper lip with those dried fingers.

"Hmph! An apprentice extraordinaire."

"Sarcasm is the seed which sows clouded thoughts and distorted realities. It hides the truth."

And yet another pause…

"So it would seem that we have learned. Which brings forth the question; a fool or one who plays the fool, thinking that he is the fool?"

"The fool would be ignorant of his knowledge, if any. The foolish man will eventually realize the truth of his ignorance and then again, he will feel the fool."

"And yet another lesson learned."

"So it would seem." My words fell as I, again into his trap.

I began, "are we armed with a wand of intuition or just grasping onto feint illusions of reality: trapped by the aspirations of the misguided past, with no hope of future revelry?"

"Time stands still."

"The heart beats no more."

"We go on, as always like before, eyes forward

pure of heart, truth…"

"… with truth comes vision."

"Yes, vision." Those grey eyes seemed to lose some of their warmth.

A fade to white, with no color.

Then a sparkle. Like that of a star on a warm summer's night.

Then to ebony, as the backbone of night. Darkness, cold, despair, fire…

Black fire…

And night consumed all.

An explosion of sunlight tore through the beaten old shades to signify the coming of another day. Clouds of dust defined the bright rays, then distorted their golden reflection into a dazzling mosaic upon all they touched.

The air clung heavily to my lungs. Their burning and aching sparked an undetermined age, that which my body had never felt before.

Eyes so tired and burning: with the salt of tears, caused by this blazing light.

I tried to focus upon that figure across from me. It seemed that for a time it wasn't there at all. Then a blink and I caught the movement of a hand. Cracked and dried, calloused fingers edged their way across the armrest of the chair, the chair in which I had sat all these countless days.

Then as a mirror, a reflection of the face stared back at me. That furrowed brow, which led to those eyes, and the path of a tear just shed. Eyes so tired their grey warmth could not smooth those lines.

I reached with my arm; limbs so brittle as if they would break, to wipe that tear. I felt that face. Skin so hard and weathered, with that hand so calloused and dried.

Then yet another tear was shed.

And the dragon sang on…

Dragon's Song

"...the humming grew louder and louder as the gold radiated the song. Reflecting light blinded the senses with its brilliant amber shimmer. High-pitched notes, momentarily broke through the melody to pierce the mind and imagination. To rape one's sanity. And to breed the fear of realization.

His eyes burned black.

Reflections of the heart and mind, together they fall.
Rapier quick. Lightning fast.
Only memory preserves. Flesh and blood dissolve.

Black fire.

Oh mother, mother.
Can your tears heal the wound?
Can I lay my head? Bleed my soul?
Will I rest forever in your arms?
Breathless wake. Sightless sound.

Burning eyes.

Fire.

Black fire.

And night consumed all...

this story was meant as an exercise in colorful description and the extreme use of semi-colons. I wanted to push each to see how they could shape the story. As in most cases, for me, the title dictates the rest. This story, like one of its predecessors, has had numerous titles. Each seemed appropriate for a period of time. Looking back, I'm not sure if any truly work though…

Crossing Boundaries

Alec sat slumped over in the dusty grey chair. Exhaustion had overcome him hours ago, but he desperately tried to stay awake. His head bobbed and weaved as he continuously lost and regained consciousness. The long tassels of his hair that repeatedly slapped his dirty and sweat covered face were streaked with shades of red. Red this time, blue last and maybe green tomorrow, any color would stand out in those long white locks.

His head snapped up quickly and with a definite, painful crack.

"Argh!'

His scream would have wakened the dead, if there had been any dead people around. No person dead or alive was foolish enough to be here though.

"I guess I'm just a dumb-ass fool then." He

spoke out loud. Nobody was near enough to hear his words or cared of his thoughts anyway.

"A fool who doesn't know when enough is enough. I had to prove it to myself; not those petty-assed theologians."

He arose from the chair and headed for the ancient fireplace. It had been at least one hundred and fifty years since the last fire had been lit. Wisps of smoke snaked out of several of the cracks in the cobble-stoned hearth filling the air with a choking gloom. His muffled coughing was almost inaudible over the sound of the burning logs being turned and twisted in the amber inferno. Fireflies of glowing embers spat toward him, catching him on the wrist in several spots. He let out with another cry as the embers smoked and ate at his flesh. The steam and stench arose to only get lost in the already pungent air.

"Enough is enough!" He shouted a repeating chorus.

He tried to convince himself that there was a purpose for his being in this gothic hellhole of decayed memories. He tried, hard as hell, to convince himself that time would indeed repeat itself; that all the answers to all of the questions would be revealed to the only person dumb enough to stand by and wait, hoping that time would not play him for the fool.

One hundred and fifty years ago the last sound was heard at Forgathé Castle. One hundred and fifty years ago a long and piercing scream sealed the mysteries; mysteries believed to be kept for countless centuries to come.

One man though, one completely foolish man on his own had decided that the walls would speak again. That he, and he alone would be the one to hear what they had to say.

It had taken Alec almost three and a half years to finally convince the Bishop of Carthé to allow his entrance. It was more the granting of a final wish, the Bishop had said.

"Death is not at good temper when awakened against its own will. For no man seeking an audience with Death can be prepared for the atrocities he will find."

"I shall remember your words, but heed not your warning." Alec had the audacity to venomously disregard the peaceful words of the cloth.

That was yesterday, this was today. Or tomorrow. How can one tell, sheltering ones own eyes behind these dark and lonely stone walls from the rays of light, that which the sun rains down.

Lonely no more.

The light from the fire reached out into the room, and yet it could not reveal its full contents. The walls seemed to stretch endlessly away; away from the amber fingers of light, feeling their way gently across the floor. Away from the golden trees waving their leaf filled branches across the ceiling so high.

He approached the darkness and paused briefly. As he turned toward the fire again he thought he caught the motion of the waves crashing into the shoreline.

A play of light.

Then towards darkness again.

His sweaty hands grasped along the walls searching out in vain, any forthcoming obstacles. His anger and his yelps of pain grew in intensity as his futile reconnaissance once again allowed an unseen object to collide violently with his knees.

"And the blind shall lead the sighted…

…the sighted to center stage.

past all the dreams,

past frantic schemes,

past reality,

affectionately…

The words of an old, almost forgotten song stung his heart and mind. As the impact of another unforeseen object bit into his knee, yet again.

Along with the pain of this new encounter between his fragile flesh and its invisible assailant came a sudden nauseating feeling. He could feel the very depths of his stomach tighten and twist. He could also feel the moistening of his pants leg as the scent of flowing blood flared in his nostrils.

Upon recognition of the severity of the situation he dropped to the floor. It was as if the sudden knowledge of injury caused a complete shutdown of his legs' ability to function.

Alec was certain that the hard landing had fractured his tail bone and he was momentarily confused as to which injury he should concern himself with first. No contest. The pulsing in his leg grew and a new wave of dizziness conceded that the growing loss of blood was too extreme a problem to ignore.

Alec tore a strip of cloth from the bottom of his shirt to fashion as a makeshift bandage. He first had to feel for the exact point on his leg where the cut was located. His hands now grasped at the wet denim to search out the flow of blood. Once found, the sticky, drying blood on his hands made tying the tourniquet increasingly difficult.

Sweat poured down his face and before realizing what he was doing, Alec reached up with his blood filled hands to wipe the sweat. The mixture of salt from sweat and blood stung his eyes and the putrid scent of drying blood, now a constant fixture on his face, turned his stomach once again.

He felt for the wall, looking for a place to lean his beaten body and breathed a heavy sigh of relief once that chore was accomplished. With his head firmly pressed to the wall, Alec slowly turned it in the direction of that unseen object.

As exhaustion consumed his body, he was certain that he could see the blood stained teeth of a grinning dragon staring back at him.

Then time and light ceased.

***

The warmth of the fire embraced Alec as the flickering of the dancing flames greeted his return to consciousness. He felt no pain from his injuries, yet he could not move either. The pleasing scent of the perfumed air swam into his senses, easing his worries and distracting him from any pain, making it unnecessary for him to move.

A faint cool breeze blew across his body, awakening him to the fact that he now laid completely naked.

Succumbing to the fact that he could not move, Alec stared at the base of the fireplace. He visually traced the mortar work of the stone hearth. Every so often the ancient stonework was cracked and an empty void was left. Those same wisps of smoke spilled through to dance with a new perfume.

He caught the movement out of the corner of his eye. But try as he might he could not turn his head to follow the movement to its source.

No need to; for the figure approached.

The shear, flowing white veils of cloth clung to her small frame. Slender hips and underdeveloped breast were wrapped in a silken cocoon. Her emerald eyes and flowing amber hair escaped the confines of yet another entrapment of cloth. One could only guess at the definition of her mouth and nose, for the vale gave no clue.

She knelt beside him and reached out to stroke his chest. Alec tried in vain to speak, but his mouth did not move. His could only close his eyes as her delicate fingers ignited every nerve in his body. Her touch continued the assault on his senses, sending him into a euphoric state of sexual arousal.

She stood once again and the moment her hands left his body, his eyes snapped quickly open. His fear that the dream had ended was washed away once his vision focused on her slender form towering above him. Her eyes bled the anticipation of the moment, as she reached behind to undo the bindings of her silken gown. The fabric slid softly off her pale skin, spiraling into a woven mound at her feet. Revealed were the soft curves of her young body. And Alec's eyes drank in the beauty of her innocence.

The warmth of her flesh fed the heat of their passion as she lowered herself on top of Alec. The intensity of their lovemaking grew with each passing stroke. The now fevered rhythm was so extreme that Alec lost all sense of the moment. Higher and higher they climbed. As the exhausting release of climax arrived, Alec's eyes shot open, only to witness the serrated edge of a sword as it flashed through the air and buried its metal tongue into the side of Innocence's head.

The horror of this vision and the reawakened pain of his injuries fueled the piercing scream Alec awoke to. His breath was quick, trying in vain to keep pace with the speeding rhythm of his heart. Tears of anguish and fear flowed from his tired eyes, all of his pity reached out to that tender image as the memory of her limp body sliding from his, sparked a new anger.

The death of Innocence played in his mind,

over and over; the reflection of flame on blade as it continually arced through the air. As metal met flesh the scene would change, only to begin again its spiraling path towards its appalling conclusion.

"Noooooo!"

His draw out scream became lost in the darkness. Alec violently pounded out his anger on the floor. He was oblivious to the damage he was doing to his hands. Dried, blood covered, skin opened, to release a fresh flood upon itself. His screams of torment continued, but the pain he felt was not for him self.

Hysteria gripped his mind. The frenzy of thoughts and the illusions of reality played vicious games with Alec's head. Every thought pulled his sanity to the brink and every image became an amplified horror to his clouded sight.

In a brief moment of clarity, he realized the only visual frame of reference to both dream and reality seemed to be the fireplace. So Alec began the painful trek to this flaming haven. He clambered to his feet, hands slipping from the flow of blood, causing him to repeatedly slide from any support he reached for. Each step was another experience in futility that echoed a crescendo of pain every time he fell to the ground. After the third of these falls, Alec was too exhausted to stand. He furiously began to crawl forward, but his efforts were to no avail. The fireplace was still an immeasurable distance away. He extended his arm in vain toward the warmth of the fire, but the loss of blood closed his eyes to his final goal.

***

Alec awoke, yet again in the arms of Innocence. Her body draped over his with the smoothness of a silken sheet and with the warmth of her skin massaging his senses.

The room, now aglow with sunlight cascading through the three large windows, revealed all of its secrets to Alec's sight. He slid from her arms and from beneath the sheets to sit and gaze upon this once darkened tomb of memories.

Darkness surely deceives. He thought as he began to survey his surroundings. The sleeping chamber seemed no bigger than most, and the walk to the fireplace, now returned to splendor, was but a few paces.

Gone was the glowing warmth of the raging inferno, the morning sun now provided the room with both light and heat. The perfect craftsmanship of the stone masonry would entomb every last wisp of the choking, grey smoke. The marble mantelpiece held a collection of golden and jeweled chalices, which caught the rays of the sun and came to life in all of their glory.

The room was filled with a bevy of antiquities; each mirroring the other with beauty and ageless grace. The meticulous artistic detail of the stone columns rose to lend their glamorous support to the ceiling. And finally, the hand carved, oak bedpost only conceded their beauty to the lovely creature that now lay between their wooden arms.

Alec turned his attention to the view through the iron-framed window. All of the images in the distance were lost in the glare of the sun reflecting through the glass. Nothing clear; just pale imitations of reality. His thoughts slipped away, searching for that reality, wondering if it would return, or if he would.

All doubts and worries ceased at the touch of Innocence. Her small hands slid from behind to embrace. He could feel the definition of her body, as she pressed tighter against him. His eyes closed as he lost himself in her again.

In his mind, images of her grace and splendor fed his thoughts with serene contentment. He turned to face her and immediately was caught in the hypnotic stare of her emerald eyes. Again he tried to speak, but realized no word, if spoken, could express the feeling he was experiencing. Instead he lowered his lips to hers and let the movement of their tongues convey his emotions.

Their embrace seemed to last an eternity; more realistically, until nightfall had again cloaked the bedchamber with its deceptive shadow.

Their bodies sank to the floor in passion once more. As the pleasure drank from their strength, they both drifted into blissful slumber.

The fires bite reflected brilliantly on the teeth of a grinning dragon.

***

Alec awoke with a start at the echoing thunder of the huge oaken door slamming shut. He stood instinctively to search out this new intrusion; only to have darkness conceal the truth once again. His thoughts quickly turned to Innocence, but as his gaze turned south to seek her sleeping form, a broad shoulder crashed into his chest and sent his already beaten and bloodied body sprawling to the base of the fireplace.

His head struck the stone base, unsettling his thoughts and causing even greater confusion. Oblivious to his body's cries of pain, Alec feverishly tried to regain his stance. His heart pounded out the fear, and the adrenaline flow shook his body uncontrollably. His legs kicked wildly outward, slipping through the lubricating pool of Innocence's blood.

Alec dove from the arcing path of the broadsword as it bit into the mortar; sending a shower of sparks through the air covering the scarlet stained image of Innocence. The vision of her illuminated form caught Alec's eyes and the pain began to swell again. He screamed out his anguish as he knelt over her still body; his tears falling to wash over the now cold and lifeless emeralds. He wanted desperately to press his lips against hers and return to the time of first encounter but the contorted mass of flesh tore at his stomach. He spun away from her form as nausea gripped his insides, causing its painful release.

Through all this, the sparking path of a sword dragged closer. The scraping metal viciously sang its song of impending death as its owner approached.

Alec wanted desperately to rise and vanquish the executioner of Innocence, but his body and will betrayed him. He barely managed the strength to raise his head and face death as the lunging metal bit into his ribcage.

His body convulsed, causing the lurching swordsman to slip violently in the growing pools of blood. The off-balanced figure spun and caught its heals on the amber mound of Innocence's hair. Flailing wildly, he landed headlong in the embracing fingers of firelight.

Confusion on the face of the fallen executioner was replaced by pain, as Alec's pain was replaced by confusion; for the face in the flame mirrored his own.

His last thought was of his taking of Innocence, and once taken, it was now gone. The death of purity to satisfy his ignorant desire for unneeded answers.

After one hundred and fifty years, the walls of Forgathé Castle spoke. Then, Alec's final scream sealed the horrors for countless centuries to come.

fôr' bōdiNG

Darkness
breeds horror into the
shattered mind...
A shadow is on the edge
of darkness,
it reaches out to pull on the
strings of your mind, leading you
into the horror that your eyesight
cannot focus upon.
You do not need to see death for it to
become a reality...
because it too, lives on the edge of sight...
in the shadows.

Of Shadows

Darkness eased its weary head upon the coastal town of Oblivion. Clouds came and went waving the moonlight across the rocks, as the waves crashed into the shoreline. The mist of the rain and the splash of the surf clung to the air, distorting any possible view. The steam of breath rose from the figure, signifying that indeed, winter was here.

Footsteps clattered and stumbled across the algae covered rock, as the mystery bobbed in and out of view. Relentlessly it went on, determined, with a definite sense of urgency.

For death has no patience.

Around the rim of the cape. To the burning lamps of the old Winchester Light-house and through the weather beaten door.

Death had arrived.

The staircase was an orange red from the years of sea air's abuse. Rust easily tore away upon any hand that grabbed the iron railing. Spiraling up, the shadow was lost in the continuous curve of the tower. The clanging echo of feet ceased only when the figure reached its goal.

The lamp room was bathed in iridescent light. Two shadows stretched out into the night, out beyond the small confinement of the room. The shadows danced in a vain effort. There will be no escape tonight.

An arm rose, the knife fell.

Death had found a home.

,elə'mentl

All Hallows

red, orange and brown
their colors change
on the ground
a pumpkin screams
a sight, no sound
witches, ghosts and goblins
a fright for all to see
haunt the sidewalks and porches
searching,
searching...

No Comfort

the Sun has set,
but the heat still oppresses,
every breath a labour,
salt stinging in eyes,
a blur of vision,
the depth of darkness
obscures the sight,
air and body fuse,
no comfort.

Lapses of Memory

Umm... I forgot
Not what was about to be said,
but what came before
The rhymes and lyrics and phrases,
the tales of olde lore
From the soliloquy of the dying man,
of poetry written in this hand
The pen, in time, now stops, alas
Umm... I forgot

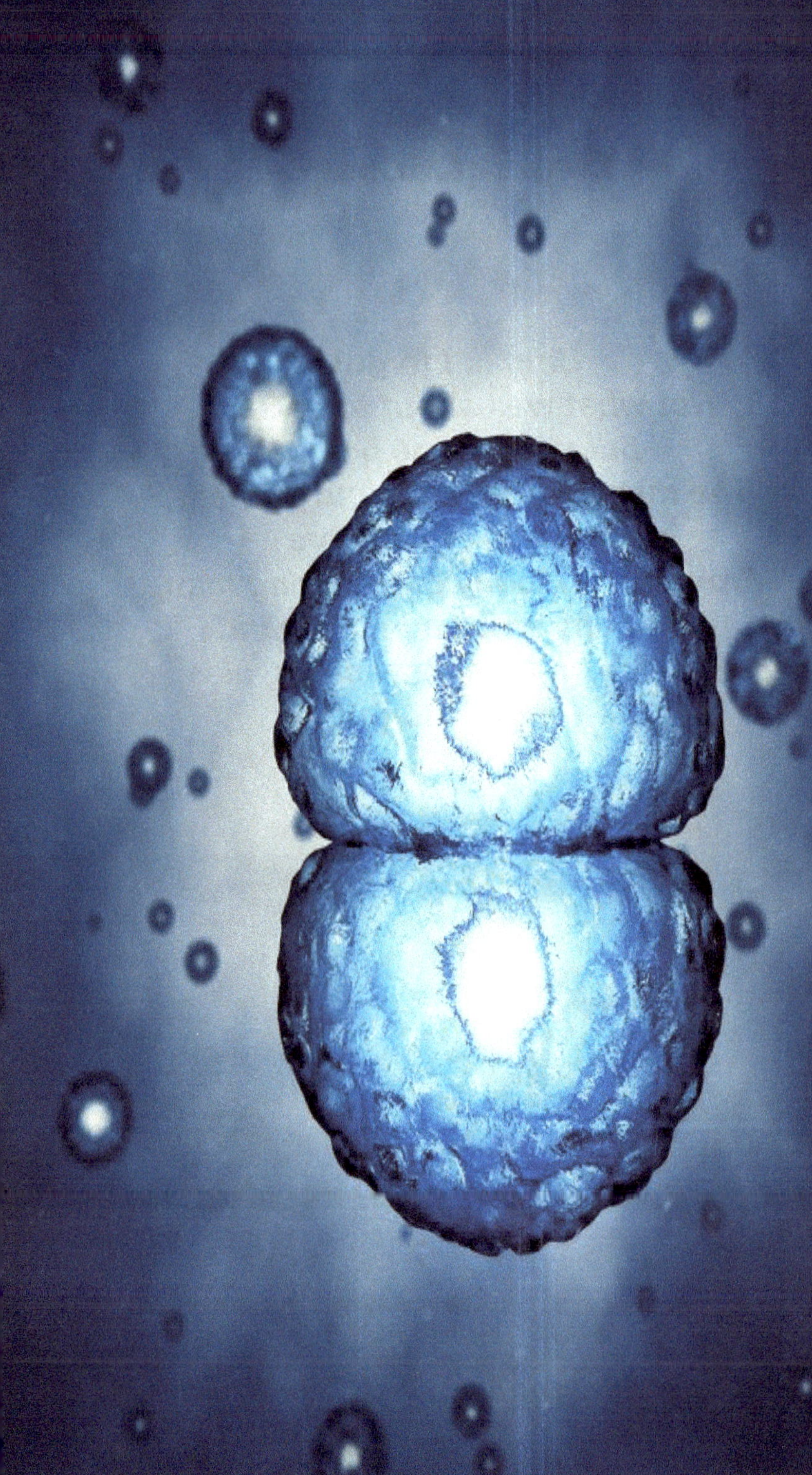

Identity Crisis

It was as if her mind just opened its proverbial eyes to her existence…

Therefore, she was.

Swimming endlessly in the dark pool of life. Knowing nothing but the fact that she was there. Sight and sound were non-existent, only the sensation of touch and the feeling of emotion were available. A growing consciousness absorbed unknown experiences and brought forth new questions to a mind pure of thought and anxious for understanding.

As time passed, each moment produced more changes, new discoveries and growth; not only of the mind, but also to the physical form. Increasing knowledge stretched its comprehension of form, size and dimension.

And she thought to herself, *I am bigger.*

With this increase in mass, came newer and more disturbing sensations, a separation of thought and feeling, dividing her being. The trembling began in the pit of her soul and increased its intensity, pulling her in every direction at once. Her mind and life's experiences, as short as it was, was being torn from her. Fear gripped her, as a tremendous crescendo tore her apart.

#

She regained consciousness as the effect of the shock that had crippled her mind, slowly subsided. A chill passed through her, awakening her emotions to the incredible loss she felt. Her body reflected the feeling. Her mass had decreased to half its previous size. Already, though, the process of growth had begun anew easing her worries.

Time continued its path forward revealing the changes that had really occurred.

She sensed another, yet the feeling of familiarity arose. Along with it came the comfort of companionship. She had not realized her prior singularity and the unrecognizable sensation that could now be called loneliness until they were replaced by the knowledge of the other. Her sister.

#

They lived together as one, sharing all experiences and growing through mutual cooperation. All of life's intricate threads weaved through their bodies and their hunger grew. Together they reached forward for more knowledge and with each new achievement their mass expanded.

Although they lived through each other, one experience had not been shared. The quickening of vibrations in the depths of their souls signaled the beginning of the separation. There was no form of preparation to convey to her sister.

It just happened.

This time, though more familiar, the results were the same. The same intense pulling of mind and experience and the same gripping fear as each was torn apart.

#

It was as if her mind had opened its proverbial eyes to their existence.

Therefore,
the four,
were.

Of Time and Space and Other Things

the winds of change flow freely through,
their curious gentle way.
and space revolves a simple sphere,
we call the Milky Way.
the time it takes to call upon,
the ones who took the time,
to find the space upon this thing,
and write this simple rhyme.

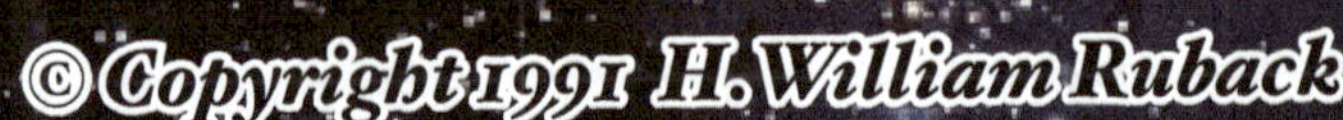

ˈdisˌkôrs

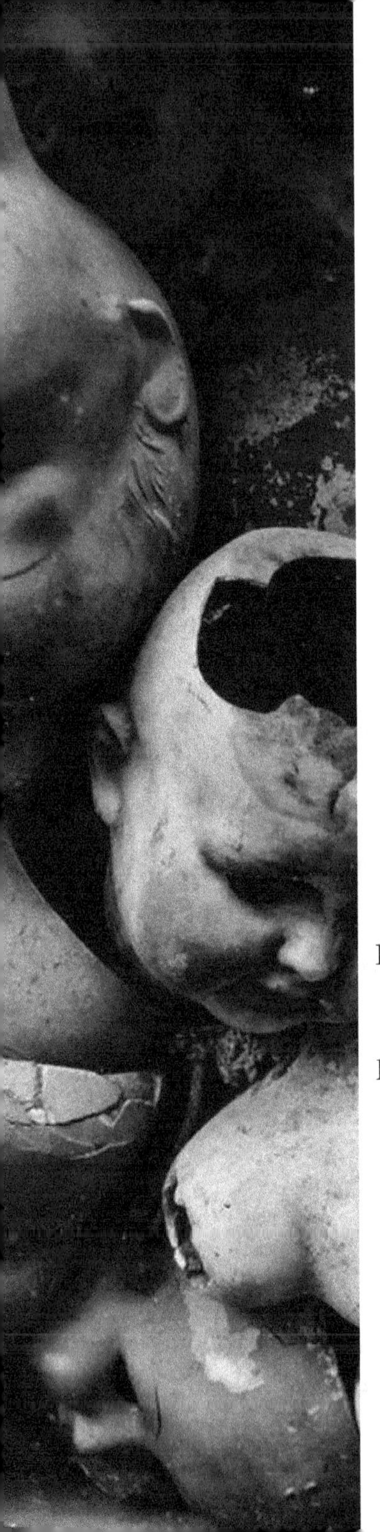

Terror I Have Found

by

Theopolis Davidity Morris

If one must look for the hidden
meaning of this paper, they will seek
forever.

If they are unlucky enough to find
what they seek, they are insane.

If they return from what they will find,
they will be destroyed.

Fear of learning that all that we held to
be, is not, can not, or will not be.

Truth through knowledge of
difference, ignorance through failure,
failure to change.

Terror, to be.

Fear that freedom to be, is not, can
not, will cease to be.

Innocence through voiced forces of
hope, ignorance through failure, failure
to change.

Terror, to be.
Insanity.

Fear of people to see, that it can not,
will not, cease to be.

Imprisonment by ignorance, ignorance
through failure, failure to change.

Terror, to be.
Insanity.
Naiveté.

Fear of feelings to be, will not be.

Terror, to be.
Humanity.

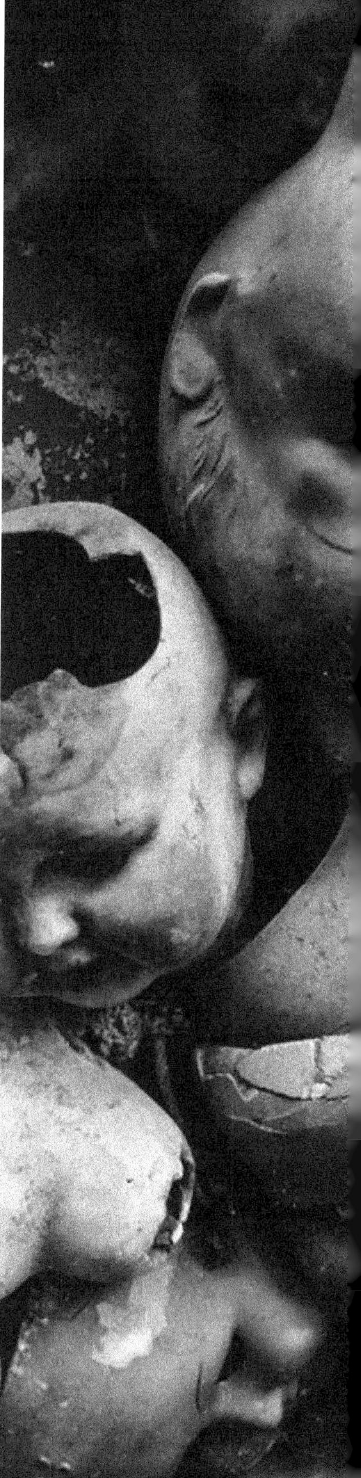

Questions Without Answers

When you realize, the truth.
Does it make it hurt any less?
Why does honesty and reality,
collide with dreams, to make things worse?
Are we all born to blind ambition,
or just resolved to live in fate?
Are we inclined to be suspicious,
or designed to expect and wait?

Question, answer answer
Question, no answer
Question, answer answer
Question without answer

Should we give in to the luxury,
that a simple mind would make?
Can we pass on new discovery,
and still progress without mistakes?

Will the lies become as subject,
to change as people are?
Can we diversify the problems
and remain as though we are?

Question, answer answer
Question, no answer
Question, answer answer
Question without answer

No answer, question question
Without answer, answered questions
No questions answered without
No answers without questions

Fear of Words

Another fear of words,
their meaning held within.
To paraphrase,
the mind's dark maze,
the moment that thought begins.

Another sound unheard,
the rhythm lost by chance.
No audible harmony,
or melody that ought to be.
No partner for this silent dance.

Another sight unseen.
Vision a matter of light, focusing just right.
Before one's eyes,
left to decide.
Follow reason or follow fright.

Another poem unread,
its soliloquy left unsaid.
Blood, thorn and rose,
lost somewhere inside the prose.
The meaning hidden by the fear of words.

Blind Child

his back is still turned
from the approaching future
his mind is disillusioned
distorted by confusion
all that's left is the burning in his eyes

life or so it seems
is an arrangement of cold realities
cold as stone and steel
no fear to ever feel
the only fear that's left is in his eyes

running from his past
his destiny at last
all that's left is the longing in his eyes

his fortune, not to seek
no risks or their plans will be endangered
their pressures at him shout
screaming to get out
darkness bleeds into the anger in his eyes

in war the battle is done
truth is not what it seems to be
his victory at stake
a judgment to be made
all you see is the pleading in his eyes

no future or no past
no destiny alas
all you see is the teardrop in his eye

Clear Canvas

paint a picture: use a lot of reds and blues
write a story: like a mystery's who's who
Clear Canvas
white page
Clear Canvas
white page
like a note that's singing softly
singing softly...
singing softly...

from the first stroke to the last
it's all the same
as you type the soliloquy out once again
increasing laugher on the stage
running around in mental disarray

white wash the Canvas
white wash the Canvas
erase the page

stroke to stroke and word by word
entering the theatre of the absurd
clearly indisposed
of creativity's flow...

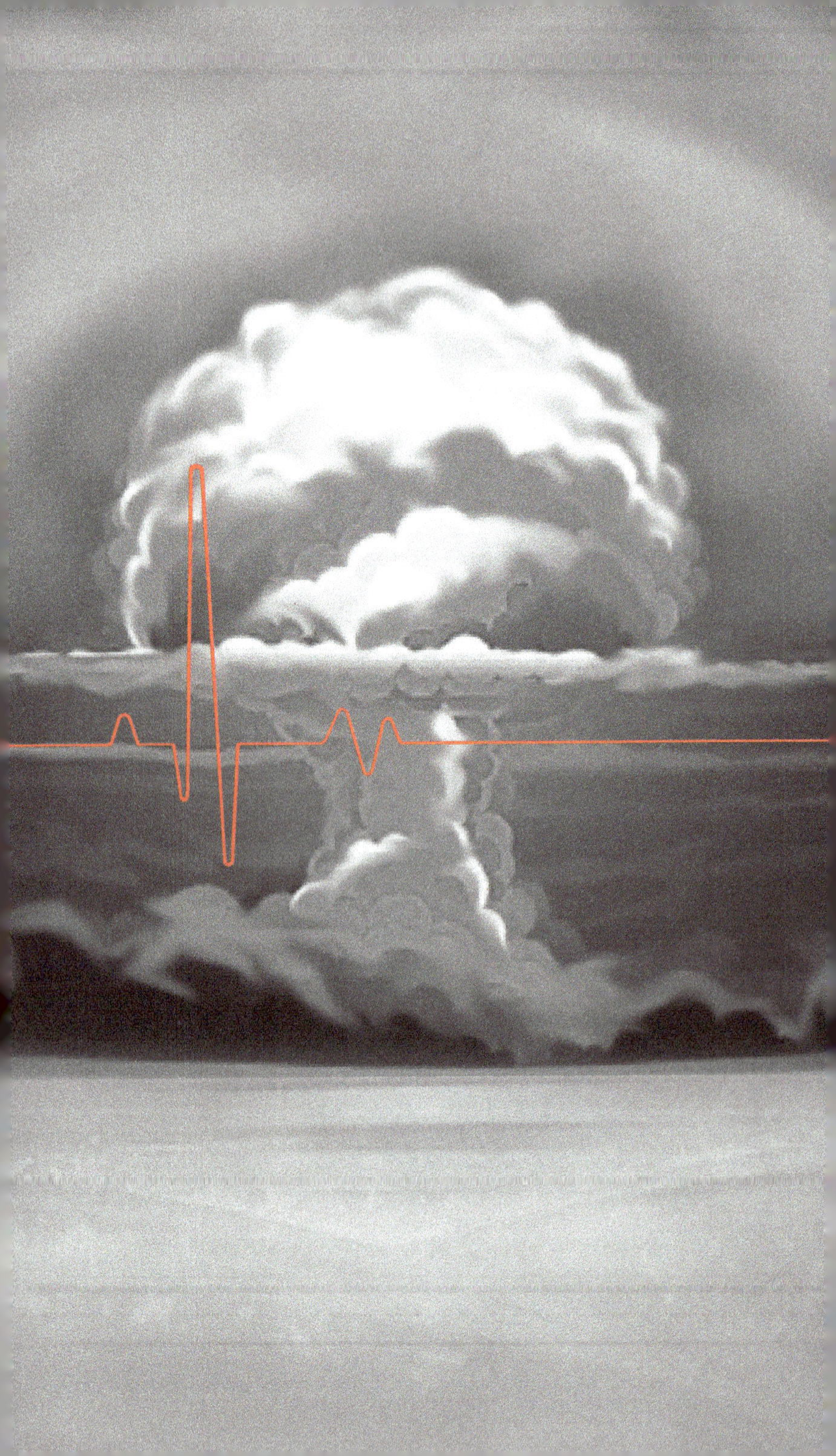

Critical Situations

The world apparent on contact zero devastation
a human deviation
of sanity
our vanity
held in tact by our lack of sensitivity
Critical
Critical
Minimal

a phantom image of corporate dehumanization
a mass computerization
the ministry
of sinistry
will resolve to dissolve all self-identity
Critical
Critical
Minimal

there's a time we finally realize
that all we see
is the world's disguise
our clouded judgment can't define the scope
as we look for dreams
through a veil of hope
Minimal
Minimal
Critical

Past Imperfect

you learn through lessons by trial
and error
all the things they should have told
you
not only the things they wanted you
to fear
past the point of no return
past the obligation you should have
kept
past imperfect
affectionately yours

time after time
and still
more yet

failure to fail their course of action
to succeed to torment against their
will
envision your vision trapped within
over and over and over and still
more yet

take back the lies you once sent
paid back the money illegally lent
feel the pain through loneliness'
restitution
fear for your soul in religious
execution

past the sorry for yourself
past the thought of should have
been

affectionately yours
perfection behind closed doors
time after time

realize... go back
clear the canvas, erase the page
imaginative demons... attack
the spotlight on center stage
council of defense... a mock
insincerity
reach out for help... retract
all false sensitivity

the blind shall lead the sighted
the sighted to center stage
past all the dreams
past frantic schemes
past reality
affectionately

past immovable force
past freewill of course
past time
and still
more yet

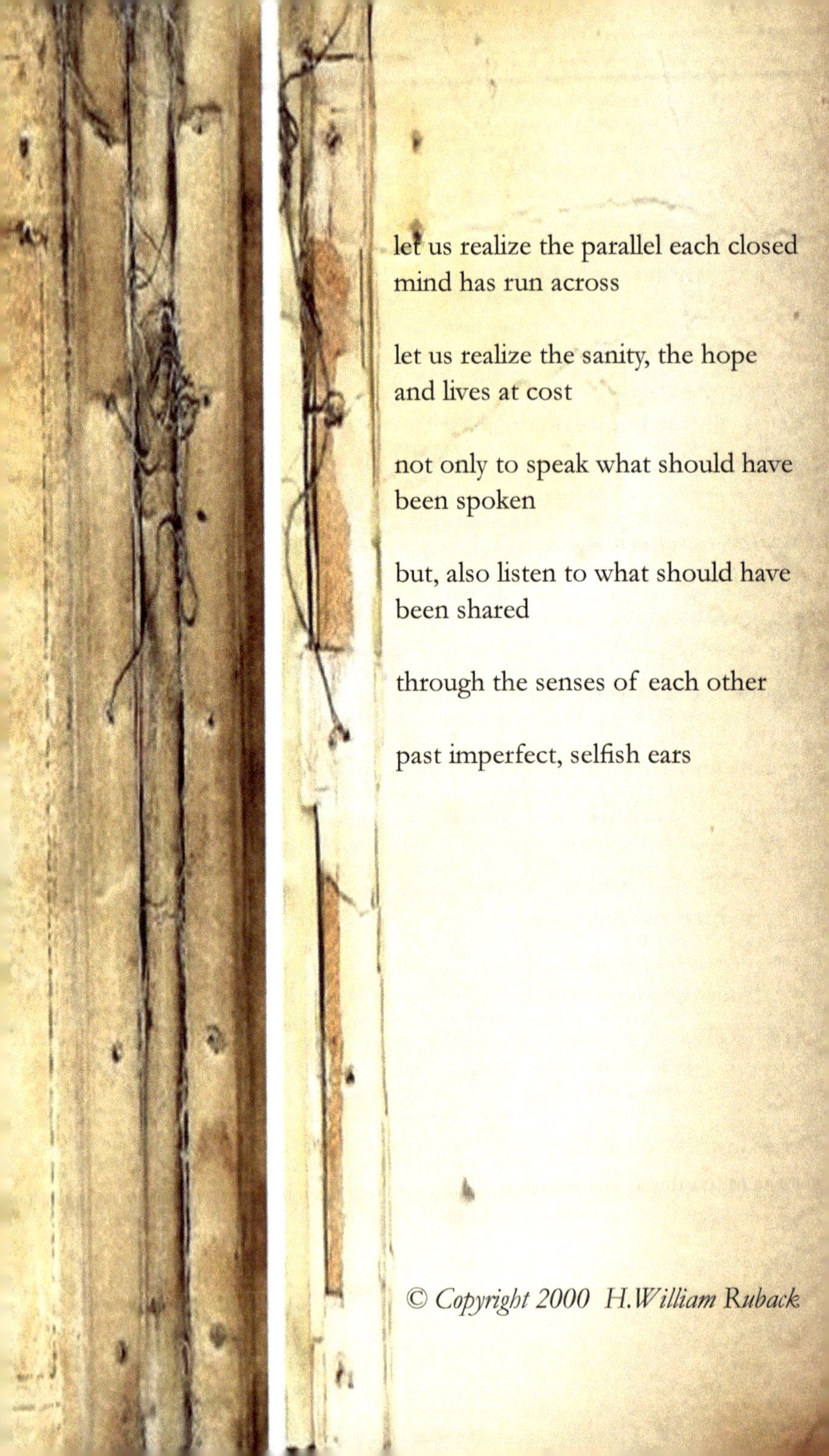

let us realize the parallel each closed
mind has run across

let us realize the sanity, the hope
and lives at cost

not only to speak what should have
been spoken

but, also listen to what should have
been shared

through the senses of each other

past imperfect, selfish ears

...and so it ends tomorrow,
the dance the Jester played.

the SHORT of it…

the next generation

this brilliant little piece comes from the mind of my eight year old. It should stand as a lesson for all those who write; as to the power your words could have in shaping the future. Several elements of my stories, still not complete, have made their influence in this piece. Enjoy!

Holy and Unholy

As portals open up from places,
Such as the heavens,
The underworld,
And new universes,
The binding magic forges,
Evil fire and holy water,
Shadowpets and archangels,
Demonic devils and powerful gods,
The almighty shall fight

looking for the Full Bottle?

the excerpt on the back cover is from the short story, "the Bottle Beside Me". Originally it was just notes to be developed into a one-man play. The more I considered performing it myself, the more descriptive it became and soon took shape, in part, as a complete story. To read the entire piece as it developes...

Go to:

http://hwilliamruback.com/the-bottle-beside-me/

About the author

Born and raised, (mostly) in Chicago, H.William Ruback has followed a creative path throughout most of his life. His love for writing was born from his passion for making music. His desire to create original art led to a thirteen-year career in the Graphics Field. His inability to escape fiction has led him back to writing and the bookselling world, as both author and seller.

Personal triumphs and tragedies have carved a sharper edge to his life. He now lives in a small town in Michigan with his wife and two sons. Sitting on a wealth of story ideas, the only demon he now faces is him-self committing the time to complete every one.

Visit him @ http://www.hwilliamruback.com
Or on
Facebook @ https://www.facebook.com/hwilliamruback

Photo Credits

Pages 1, 9, 23, 51, 56, 65: (altered) Original Image © Valeriy Gayevyy@123rf.com
Page 6: "Transit of Venus" photo © 2013 H.William Ruback
Page 10: Original background Image © loraliv@123rf.com
Page 10: Original inset Image (buildings) © Joy Prescott@123rf.com
Page 17: (altered) Original background Image © Ionut Dan Popescu@123rf.com
Page 17: Original inset Image © Allyson Kitts@123rf.com
Page 18: Original background Image © Gordon Poropat@123rf.com
Page 18: Original inset Image © Olga Drozdova@123rf.com
Page 19: (altered) Original Image © Valerii Sidelnykov@123rf.com
Page 22: "Warrior's Touch" photo © 2014 Steve LeBel
Page 22: (altered) Original background Image © Vadim Shkirenko@123rf.com
Page 24: "Mandrake and Me" sketch © 1996 Michael Bricis
Page 24: Original background Image © Fernando Cortes De Pablo@123rf.com
Page 36: (altered) Original Image © Simone Gatterwe@123rf.com
Page 37: Original Image © Weerayut Kongsombut@123rf.com
Page 38: (altered) Original Image © misha@123rf.com
Page 39 - 50: (altered) Original Image © arsgera@123rf.com
Pages 52, 53: (altered) Original Image © speedfighter@123rf.com
Page 54: Original Image © hypermania2@123rf.com
Page 57: Original Image © Olga Drozdova@123rf.com
Page 58: Original Image © Ben Goode@123rf.com
Page 59: (altered) Original Image © PÃ©ter Gudella@123rf.com
Page 60 - 63: (altered) Original Image © nobeastsofierce@123rf.com
Page 64: Original Image © eevl@123rf.com
Pages 66, 67: (altered) Original Image © aarstudio@123rf.com
Pages 68, 69: (altered) Original Image © Евгений Косцов@123rf.com
Page 70: Original Image © natika@123rf.com
Page 71: (altered) Original Image © illustrart@123rf.com
Page 72: Original Image © donatas1205@123rf.com
Page 73: Original Image © Piotr Palacki@123rf.com
Page 74: (altered) Original Image © Maksim Pasko @123rf.com
Page 74: (altered) Original Image © Andrea Crisante @123rf.com
Page 76 - 78: Original Image © Igor Korionov @123rf.com
Page 79: (altered) Original Image © anyka @123rf.com
Page 80: "Acid Rain" ink on vellum, © 1989 H.William Ruback
Page 82: Original Image © Aleksandr Steblovskiy @123rf.com
Page 83: Photo of the author © 1996 Christine M. Ruback
Page 84: Original Image © Gordan Poropat @123rf.com

www.ingramcontent.com/pod-product-compliance
Lightning Source LLC
Chambersburg PA
CBHW070607310726
48982CB00001B/4
9780991055470